Elizabeth's Song

BEYOND
WORDS
Publishing
I N C

ℰLIZABETH'S SONG is a fictionalized story inspired by actual events that occurred during the life of Elizabeth Cotten.

Beyond Words Publishing, Inc.
20827 N.W. Cornell Road, Suite 500
Hillsboro, Oregon 97124-9808
503-531-8700

Editor: Michelle Roehm
Book Design: Dorral Lukas, Barbara Mann, and JoAnne Olson

Printed in Korea
Distributed to the book trade by Publishers Group West

Library of Congress Cataloging-in-Publication Data

Wenberg, Michael.
    Elizabeth's song / written by Michael Wenberg ; illustrated by Cornelius Van Wright.
        p. cm.
    Summary: A fictionalized account of how an eleven-year-old girl, Elizabeth "Libba" Cotten, saved to buy her first guitar and composed the popular folksong, "Freight Train."
Includes a brief summary of her life's work and awards.
    ISBN 1-58270-069-9
    1. Cotten, Elizabeth—Juvenile fiction. 2. Folk singers—United States—Biography—Juvenile fiction. [1. Cotten, Elizabeth—Fiction. 2. Singers—Fiction. 3. Folk music—Fiction.] I. Van Wright, Cornelius, ill. II. Title.

PZ7.W4689 El 2002
[Fic]—dc21

2001058954

The corporate mission of Beyond Words Publishing, Inc:
Inspire to Integrity

Elizabeth's Song

For Sandy
—MICHAEL WENBERG

To my beloved Ying-Hwa
—CORNELIUS VAN WRIGHT

BEYOND
WORDS
Publishing

*I*T WAS SPRINGTIME IN CHAPEL HILL, NORTH Carolina. The year was 1903.

In a small yellow house by the railroad tracks, a young girl named Elizabeth sat in the middle of the cramped, hot kitchen. She was admiring the graceful way her mother worked in front of the fire-blackened wood stove.

She was also thinking about a piano.

"Mama?" Elizabeth said.

"Yes, Sugar," her mother replied.

"Are you sure we can't get a piano?"

"You know we can't afford one," her mother said.

"But Mama . . ."

"Since you're so riled up to play an instrument," her mother interrupted, "why don't you just borrow your brother's guitar like before?"

"He won't let me," Elizabeth said, frowning.

"And why not?"

"I keep bustin' strings," she said, adding quickly, "but I don't mean to."

"Well, maybe it's high time you earn some money and buy a guitar of your very own," her mother suggested.

"But . . . but . . . how?" Elizabeth sputtered.

Her mother thought for a moment. "Tomorrow I'm makin' three pecan pies for Miz Bartlett. I know you're shy, but you come along when I deliver 'em. We'll see if she has somethin' a good, hard worker like yourself can do."

"I . . . I 'spose I can do that," Elizabeth said.

"Now that we got that put to bed," her mother said with a tired chuckle, "why don't you shoo outside and play, and let me get back to cookin'." She gave Elizabeth a hug and then pushed her gently toward the back door.

*I*NSTEAD OF PLAYING, ELIZABETH RAN BESIDE THE train tracks until she came to a small, grass-covered hill—her secret place.

She scrambled to the top to wait for her brother and her father. From here she would see them coming home from work at the nearby rock quarry.

It wasn't long before Elizabeth heard the sound of thunder. It was a low-pitched rumble that she felt in her stomach more than she heard. Elizabeth knew it wasn't a storm coming but something just as magnificent—a freight train.

As the train pulled closer, the hill started shaking. Elizabeth closed her eyes and began to sing, keeping time with the approaching *clickity-clack* of the train's wheels:

Freight train, freight train, run so fast.
Freight train, freight train, run so fast . . .

There was a sudden rush of wind and sound, like a brass band gone wild, as the train burst past her. And then, just as quickly, it was gone, its music fading and dropping slowly like a forgotten promise.

$\mathcal{E}$LIZABETH OPENED HER EYES AND SHRIEKED so loudly that two crows were scared out of the nearby tree.

In the middle of the trestle, she could see the head and shoulders of some poor man who must have been caught on the tracks and run down by the train.

Elizabeth shrieked again when the dead man jumped to his feet, the rest of his body appearing magically from the gap between the railroad ties. She watched him, open-mouthed with surprise, as he brushed off his clothes and strode confidently from tie to tie like he was taking a Sunday walk. It was only when he was closer that Elizabeth realized the man was her brother, Louis, his face lit up by a big smile.

"*A*RE YOU CRAZY?" ELIZABETH YELLED AT HIM WHEN he scrambled up the hill.

Louis checked himself, as if to make sure. "Nope," he said, giving her one of his lopsided grins. "I'm just havin' fun. I wait until that ol' Number 9 gets close, then I drop down between the ties and hang there like one of those circus trapeze artists. When it's by, I swing back up."

"But you coulda got yourself killed dead!" Elizabeth cried, so upset she was having trouble holding back her tears.

"Nahhhhh," Louis said. "I'm real careful." He pulled Elizabeth to her feet. "Daddy's gonna be awhile. Let's head home."

As they walked along the tracks, Elizabeth's sniffles stopped almost immediately. When Louis glanced down, she was staring up at him, her hand clamped tightly across her mouth.

"Well, Little Sis, what is it?" Louis asked. "Better get it out before you pop like a balloon."

"I was thinkin'," Elizabeth said, a sly smile on her lips, "that Mama will be very mad when she hears what you've been doin'."

"Whoo-ee," Louis whistled with admiration. "I can guess where this is goin'."

"Now 'spose we keep my havin' fun a little secret, just 'tween you and me? And as long as you keep my secret, 'spose I let you play my guitar when I'm at work?"

Elizabeth clapped her hands with excitement. "Deal," she said, before Louis could change his mind. It wasn't a piano or a guitar of her own, but it would do for now. "Shakin' makes it official."

"Just don't break any more strings," grumbled Louis, grabbing her hand firmly. "They don't grow on trees, you know."

"Cross my heart," Elizabeth promised.

STARTING THE VERY NEXT DAY, ELIZABETH BEGAN playing Louis's guitar whenever he was gone. At first, she tried playing it right-handed, the way he had shown her before. But Elizabeth was left-handed, and playing the guitar Louis's way just didn't feel right.

"It's like I'm tryin' to pet a cat backwards," she explained to her brother that evening.

"But it's the right way," Louis insisted. "You gotta keep tryin'."

"It may be the right way for you," Elizabeth said stubbornly, "but not for me. I'm just gonna have to play this my way."

From then on, Elizabeth's way was playing the guitar left-handed and upside down. The more she played, the easier it became. Before long, her fingers seemed to know what to do all by themselves.

$\mathcal{E}$VEN THOUGH SHE COULD PLAY LOUIS'S guitar now, Elizabeth wanted to buy a guitar of her own. The idea was always hanging there in the back of her mind like a lost dog. Whenever Elizabeth wasn't at school or helping her mother or making up a song, she was going door to door, looking for work.

At one of the first places Elizabeth tried, a woman stepped out on the porch, put her hands on her hips, and said, "What can a little girl like you do?"

Elizabeth was ready. "I can sweep the kitchen," she fired back, "set the table, bring in wood, make a fire, watch your kids, scrub vegetables, make beds, dust the furniture, shake rugs . . ."

She said so many things all in one breath that the woman finally threw up her hands and surrendered. "Come on in," she laughed, "and we'll talk."

Wherever she worked, Elizabeth's favorite job was sweeping the porch. It gave her a chance to sing, keeping time to the music with the rhythmic swish of the broom: "*Freight train*—swish—*freight train*—swish—*run so fast*—swish-swish . . ."

Sometimes she got so carried away with her song that she'd end up sweeping the porch twice.

Elizabeth's odd jobs never made her much money. And when she was stacking wood in the hot sun or hauling a heavy basket of potatoes out of a garden or changing the diaper on a screaming baby, it almost didn't seem worth it. But month after month, those pennies added up.

*T*HAT NIGHT, ELIZABETH LAY IN bed, listening to the music coming from the front porch. Her brother and some neighbors were playing a tune called "Wilson Rag."

When the notes from the banjo, fiddle, and guitars died out, the group switched to an old church song. She heard her mother's rich, strong voice joining in. "*What a friend we have in Jesus . . . ,*" she sang.

Elizabeth smiled to herself in the darkness. She pulled the quilt up tight beneath her chin, her fingers dancing along with the notes of her mother's song.

After awhile, when it was finally quiet, Elizabeth heard the far-off trumpet wail of a freight train, restless and prowling the tracks like some half-tamed beast.

"*Freight train, freight train, run so fast . . . ,*" Elizabeth chanted sleepily to herself.

ONE EVENING, ELIZABETH BANGED THROUGH THE front door. She was tired, dirty, and scratched up from trimming rose bushes. But the shiny nickel in her pocket made her smile.

Once inside, however, Elizabeth realized that something was wrong. Her mother was sitting in her rocking chair, hands covering her face. Her father stood in the kitchen doorway, his clothes still dusty from the quarry, his mouth a thin line. Louis was leaning against the wall, arms across his chest, looking angry and sad at the same time.

"He's goin' away north," her mother said softly.

"Louis?" Elizabeth whispered. She looked at her brother with disbelief, hoping her mother was wrong, hoping she hadn't heard it right.

"I'm leavin'," Louis admitted, the words starting slowly and then tumbling out. "Tonight. I'm taking the train north. Everybody's goin'. They say there's lotsa work up there. Opportunities. New York City's the place. There's nothin' for me here."

Shame clouded his face as he realized what he had said. "I didn't mean . . ." he stammered, but then he gave up. One look at Elizabeth's stricken face and he shook his head with regret, "Sorry, Little Sis, but I'll be takin' my guitar with me."

"Oh," Elizabeth squeaked. Her hands fluttered like butterflies as she looked from Louis to her mother and father and then back to Louis. He held her gaze for a moment and then shrugged and looked away. That was enough to break the spell. Elizabeth clenched her hands, spun on her heels, and raced back out into the night.

SHE DIDN'T GO FAR—JUST ALONG THE TRACKS TO the grassy hill by the trestle—her place.

That's where Louis found her.

"I knew you'd be here," he said, dropping his duffel bag onto the ground.

"Do you have to go?" Elizabeth pleaded, wiping the tears from her face with the back of her hand.

Louis took a deep breath, looking up at the dark sky. "Yeah, Sis," he said finally. "It's time."

"Why?" Elizabeth said, not ready to give up. "You got work at the quarry . . ."

Louis shook his head, his mouth working as he tried to find the words. He knelt down next to her. "You'll understand soon enough. I want more than just working at the quarry the rest of my life. There's so much to see out there . . ."

A TRAIN WHISTLED IN THE DISTANCE.

"That'll be the Number 9," Louis said. He pinched her on the cheek. "Have I told you that I'm proud of you?"

Elizabeth shook her head.

"Well, I am. You're workin' so hard. Before you know it, you're gonna have your own guitar."

Elizabeth didn't say anything. At that moment, she was willing to give up music forever if that would keep Louis from going away.

"Promise to take care of Mama for me?" Louis asked gently.

Elizabeth nodded.

Louis held out his hand. "Shakin' makes it official," he said with a wink.

Elizabeth grabbed his hand and held it tight. "Cross my heart," she whispered fiercely.

Louis leaned down and kissed her on the forehead, and then he was gone.

ℰLIZABETH SAT THERE FOR A LONG WHILE, rocking back and forth, watching the trains go by. After awhile, she began singing, her fingers moving along like she was playing a guitar:

Freight train, freight train, run so fast.
Please don't tell what train I'm on.
They won't know what route I've gone.

As Elizabeth sang, she thought about Louis. She could almost see him, standing in an open boxcar, the wind ripping and tugging at his clothes as the freight train screamed north into the night.

She also thought about the pennies, nickels, and dimes she had saved in the bag beneath her pillow. Just forty-two cents. Not nearly enough for a guitar—not yet.

She wasn't about to give up. She would just work harder.

She would keep Louis proud of her.

In the meantime, she'd just have to make do. There was always the old cornstalk fiddle under her bed and paper on a comb. She could even keep time to her songs with the washboard in the tub outside.

She'd make do.

NINE MONTHS LATER, ELIZABETH AND her mother stepped into the cool interior of McDougal's Dry Goods and Sundries.

"What can I do for you fine ladies?" Alexander McDougal said as he approached the counter.

Elizabeth smiled broadly, "I'm here to buy a Stella," she said.

"You mean that guitar I've seen you gawking at all year?" McDougal asked.

"Yes sir," Elizabeth said.

"Do you have enough money?" Elizabeth didn't notice the wink that McDougal gave her mother.

"Yes sir, I do," Elizabeth said proudly. She opened the bag she had kept under her pillow. The coins tumbled out onto the counter. Elizabeth began counting.

McDougal chuckled. "No need for that," he said. "How much do you have?"

"Exactly three dollars and seventy-five cents," Elizabeth boasted.

"Hmmm," McDougal said, a puzzled look on his face. "I don't rightly recall just what that Stella costs . . ."

"Three dollars and seventy-five cents!" Elizabeth burst out.

"So it does," McDougal chuckled as he pulled down the instrument. "So it does."

Elizabeth held her breath. Up close, the guitar was even more beautiful than she had imagined. She stroked the back of it, its finish smooth as glass, and then ran her fingers lightly up the neck.

"You sure you know what to do with this thing?" McDougal asked, breaking her spell.

"Yes, sir," Elizabeth answered, giving him her biggest grin and then dancing over to her mother's side. "Can we go now?" she begged. "Please?"

*T*HAT NIGHT, THE SAD WAIL OF A FREIGHT TRAIN SOARED into the dark sky.

"Time for bed, Sugar," her mother announced. Elizabeth had been playing her new guitar ever since they had gotten home hours before.

"Those train whistles always makes me think of Louis," Elizabeth said wistfully.

"Me, too," her mother added with a sigh.

"You think he's doing all right, Mama?"

"I pray every night that he is," she said, staring so fiercely out the darkened window that Elizabeth wondered if she was trying to see all the way to New York City.

"Before I tuck you in, you wanna play me some of that song you been workin' on all night?"

Elizabeth nodded. "Yes'm. I wrote it for Louis. I call it 'Freight Train.'"

She picked the strings of the guitar, soft and sweet. After a few moments, she began to sing:

> *Freight train, freight train, run so fast.*
> *Freight train, freight train, run so fast.*
> *Please don't tell what train I'm on.*
> *They won't know what route I've gone.*

> *When I am dead and in my grave*
> *No more good times here I crave*
> *Place the stones at my head and feet*
> *Tell them all that I've gone to sleep.*

> *When I die, Lorde, bury me deep*
> *Way down on old Chestnut Street*
> *So I can hear old Number 9*
> *As she comes rolling by.*

When I die, Lorde, bury me deep
Way down on old Chestnut Street
Place the stones at my head and feet
Tell them all that I've gone to sleep.

EPILOGUE

*E*lizabeth "Libba" Cotten was born in Chapel Hill, North Carolina, in 1893. She is best known for "Freight Train," a song she wrote in 1904 when she was just eleven years old. Her music has been played and recorded by many famous musicians, including Pete Seeger; John Lennon; Joan Baez; Peter, Paul and Mary; and even the Grateful Dead.

Elizabeth is also known for her unique style of guitar playing. She played a regular right-handed guitar upside down and left-handed, with the bass string on the bottom.

Despite Elizabeth's talent, musical success didn't come until late in her life. Beginning in her mid-teens and continuing for the next thirty years, she spent her time and energy raising a family and making a living as a housekeeper. Her guitar was mostly silent during this period. Then, in the mid-1940s, Elizabeth had a chance meeting with Ruth Crawford Seeger, stepmother of well-known folksinger Pete Seeger. As her friendship with the Seeger family grew, so did Elizabeth's desire to return to the music she loved.

Encouraged by her friends, Elizabeth began playing again and released her first album in 1958. She had her first public performance a year afterward at the age of sixty-seven!

Late in her life Elizabeth finally got the attention she deserved, receiving many honors, including a Grammy Award and recognition by the Smithsonian Institution and the National Endowment for the Arts, among others. The Libba Cotten Conservancy was founded to teach people about Elizabeth's life and music, and the city of Syracuse, New York, where she lived at the end of her life, even named a park after her: "Libba Cotten Grove."

Elizabeth Cotten passed away on June 29, 1987.

If you'd like to hear Elizabeth Cotten sing and play the guitar, her CDs are widely available at retail and on-line music stores. For tips on using this book in the classroom and more about Elizabeth Cotten, go to elizabeths-song.com.